TRIANGULAR TREV
and the
SHAPE IDOLS

To Izzy
Best Wishes,
Christina Gabbitas :)

CHRISTINA GABBITAS

illustrated by
SIMON COOPER

Triangular Trev takes a walk in the park,
counting his very large paces.
He stops to tie his
eight holed laces.

He jumps up and bumps into his friend Isosceles Irene,
who is walking and humming in a daydream.

"Look where you are going," says Triangular Trev.
"I nearly lost my balance and banged my head!"

"I'm so sorry," says Isosceles Irene,
"I really didn't mean to cause a scene."

"No problem!
What's that tune
you were humming?
It sounded cool."

"I want to enter the
Band Idol competition,
but don't want to
sound like a fool!"

"No way!" says Triangular Trev. "How about we get
together with our other friends who love music?
We all have a talent, so let's use it!"

"Let's find Rectangular Reg and Equilateral Eric,
when they get together they sound epic!"

Triangular Trev and
Isosceles Irene go
on a mission to find
their musical mates,
to form a band and
organise practice
dates.

4

On their way through the park they hear
some noise coming from the bandstand.
They spot Nonagon Norma with a
tambourine in her hand.

"I love to sing, I love to shout,
having fun and dancing about."

"Over here," shouts Nonagon Norma,
"I am composing a song for the Band Idol competition.
I am hoping to "nail it" with my first audition."

Isosceles Irene says,
"Well that's what we were hoping to do.
Can we team up with you?"

"Yes," says Triangular Trev.
"We were hoping that the rest of our team
could help us all fulfil our dream!"

"That sounds like a plan!
What are we waiting for?
Let's join the rest of
the clan!"

Triangular Trev, Isosceles Irene and
Nonagon Norma carry on walking through Oval Tree Park.
Approaching the pond they hear a very loud bark.

"Come back Trigonometry!"
shouts a panicky looking figure holding a bone.

"It's Perpendicular Peri," says
Nonagon Norma with an excited tone.

"Over here! I'm with Triangular Trev and
Isosceles Irene, and your dog Trigonometry."

"Keep hold of him for me with
his floppy right ear," shouts
Perpendicular Peri.

"Thanks Nonagon Norma. Trigonometry's always running off on his own."

"We are forming a band to enter Band Idol and I wondered if you would play your saxophone?" says Nonagon Norma.

"Play?! What?! Yes, of course I would. I will need to take Trig home for his rest, before he becomes a pest!"

"Okay, meet us at Triangular Trev's house. It's 180 Degree Close, just off Spherical Street."

Perpendicular Peri skips away with Trig, on her size seven feet.

Triangular Trev, Isosceles Irene, Nonagon Norma and Perpendicular Peri just need two more members to complete their team to help them fulfil their Band Idol dream.

As they walk out of Oval Tree Park, they spot Horizontal Horatio and Rectangular Reg standing by an hexagonal hedge.

Triangular Trev shouts, "Hey look who it is! Rectangular Reg and Horizontal Horatio." They all give one another a big high five and a huge hello.

"It's great to see you. What are you both up to?"

Rectangular Reg replies, "We were just discussing the number of keys on a keyboard and xylophone, and the differences in their sound and tone."

"My keyboard has fifty-two white keys and thirty-six black keys."

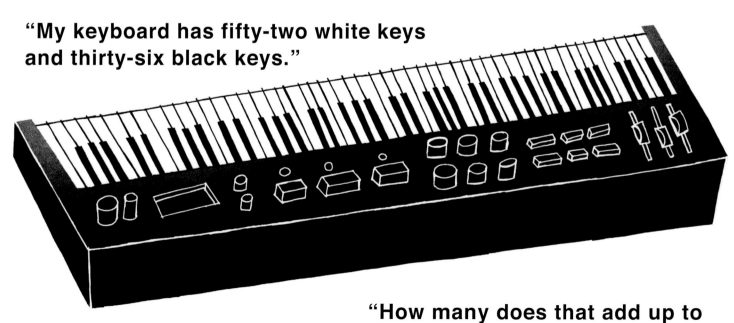

"How many does that add up to Rectangular Reg, if you please?" replies Horizontal Horatio.

Isosceles Irene butts in,
"I do believe that adds up to eighty-eight altogether."

"WOW! Isosceles Irene,
you were quick to answer that.
You are very clever,"
says Nonagon Norma.

"That's also a lot of keys to play, would you like to
join our band to enter the Band Idol competition?
We want to impress the judges at our audition."

"That sounds like a fantastic idea,"
says Rectangular Reg. "Count me
in too," says Horizontal Horatio.
"How could we possibly say no!"

"All we need now," says Triangular Trev,
"is Equilateral Eric.
His recording studio is epic!"

"Let's make our way to his house
on Pythagoras Avenue,
Hypotenuse House,
it's just one hundred
metres away."

PYTHAGORAS AVE

"Follow me everyone, walk this way."

They all arrive at Equilateral Eric's house,
press the doorbell and listen to its rhythmic chime,
all hoping that Equilateral Eric will be
interested in hitting the big time!

Equilateral Eric opens the door with
his headphones around his neck.
"Hi everyone! I've just been mixing some
music on my vinyl record deck."

"That sounds really cool,"
says Triangular Trev.
"Can we listen?"

"We are all
hoping that with your expertise,
you can help us get into first position
when we enter the Band Idol Competition."

"Sounds out there guys.
I would love to be part of the team.
We could be the best thing the competition has ever seen!"

They all begin to share their ideas of musical styles,
laughing and joking with happy smiles.

Nonagon Norma likes pop,
she thinks it top!

Isosceles Irene likes
African drumming.
You can often hear
her humming!

Perpendicular Peri
likes jazz;
she says her saxophone
adds pizazz!

Horizontal Horatio likes classical,
he says it's marvellously magical!

Equilateral Eric likes
listening to rap.
He really is
a cool chap!

Triangular Trev
likes to sing country.
He plays guitar and
makes it sound funky!

Rectangular Reg
likes electronic;
he thinks his keyboard
is supersonic!

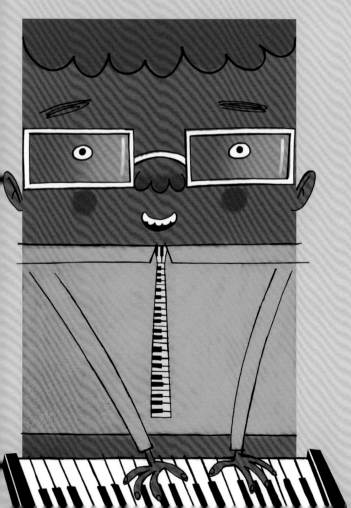

The contest is now only hours away.
They've worked hard, rehearsing every day.
This is their big chance to get through to the final.
Their main threat is The Cones,
the favourites to win Band Idol.

They arrive at the Probability Theatre
with their instruments in hand.
As they walk through the door
Perpendicular Peri says,
"Wow! How grand."

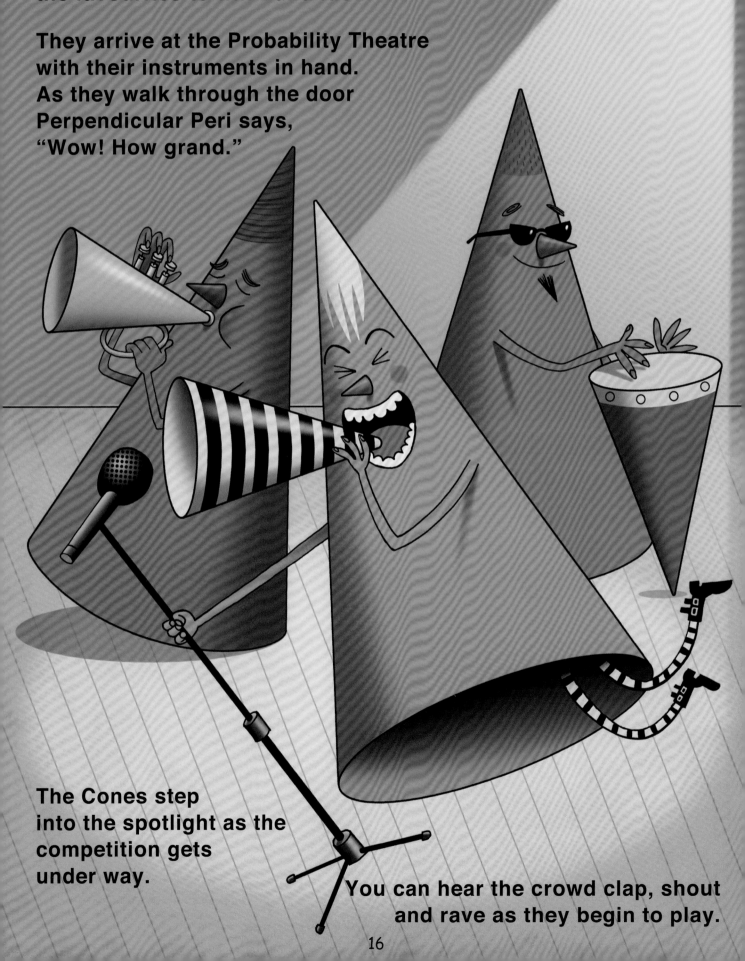

The Cones step
into the spotlight as the
competition gets
under way.

You can hear the crowd clap, shout
and rave as they begin to play.

16

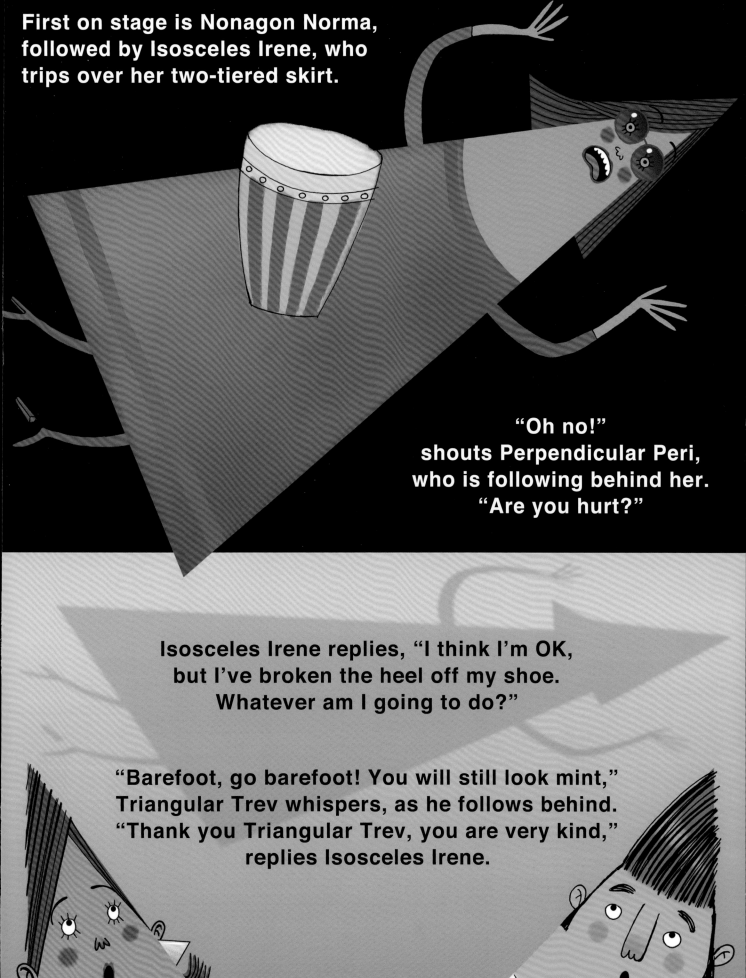

First on stage is Nonagon Norma, followed by Isosceles Irene, who trips over her two-tiered skirt.

"Oh no!" shouts Perpendicular Peri, who is following behind her. "Are you hurt?"

Isosceles Irene replies, "I think I'm OK, but I've broken the heel off my shoe. Whatever am I going to do?"

"Barefoot, go barefoot! You will still look mint," Triangular Trev whispers, as he follows behind. "Thank you Triangular Trev, you are very kind," replies Isosceles Irene.

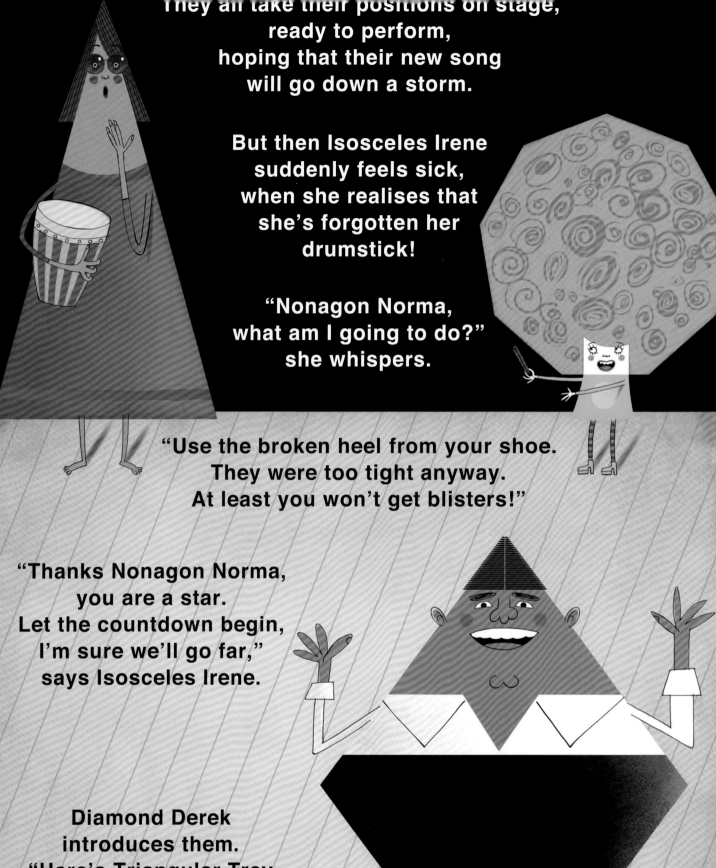

They all take their positions on stage,
ready to perform,
hoping that their new song
will go down a storm.

But then Isosceles Irene
suddenly feels sick,
when she realises that
she's forgotten her
drumstick!

"Nonagon Norma,
what am I going to do?"
she whispers.

"Use the broken heel from your shoe.
They were too tight anyway.
At least you won't get blisters!"

"Thanks Nonagon Norma,
you are a star.
Let the countdown begin,
I'm sure we'll go far,"
says Isosceles Irene.

Diamond Derek
introduces them.
"Here's Triangular Trev
and the Shape Idols!
We wish you all the best
against your rivals."

We are here to entertain you.
To let you know a little about us and what we do.
We are the shape of things to come,
born to entertain and have fun.

Here's Nonagon Norma...
My favourite number is nine.
I sing and play the tambourine to the beat in time.
We are all crazy about numbers, timing and beats.
We like to get everybody moving out of their seats.
We like to add, subtract and sing our times tables too.
Numbers and beats make it easy to do.

Here's Triangular Trev...
I have three angles, three straight sides and I play guitar.
My Auntie Polygon says I will go far.
We hope you enjoy the Band Idol song.
It's a great tune for you to sing along.

Here's Rectangular Reg...

I have one flat face with four small edges,
Two long and two short sides.
I'm hoping to impress the judges.
I play the keyboard with eighty-eight keys
and stand at the back.
I mix all the instruments together
and concentrate on the backing track.

Equilateral Eric's the name...

And all my sides are the same.
I play triangle and sing
backing vocals too.
My timing is perfect,
I know exactly
what to do!

Here's Isosceles Irene...

I have two equal angles
and two sides of equal length.
My colourful, positive character
goes from strength to strength.
I play the drum and dance to the beat.
You can hear the sound of my tapping feet.

Here's Perpendicular Peri...

Two of my lines cross at right angles.
See my bling, bling earrings and how they dangle.
I play a tenor saxophone that has thirty-two keys.
My family think that I'm the bee's knees!

Here's Horizontal Horatio...

I like swaying
from side to side
with my xylophone.
When I play music,
I'm in the zone.

Right to left
and left to right.
Playing long and loud
into the night!

We've been
practicing hard for the
Band Idol competition,
to help us all achieve
our ambition.

We are the shape of things to come,
born to entertain and have fun.
We hope you like who we are
and hope that we are the best by far.

There is cheering, smiling and clapping in abundance,
and a standing ovation from the audience.

Diamond Derek announces the winner as he takes to the stage,
whilst everyone is having a rave.
He begins to announce the results of the night
it's Triangular Trev and the Shape Idols who have won the fight!

"Hooray, hooray!
All our hard work paid off. We are a winning team.
We helped one another achieve our dream!"

Triangular Trev And The Shape Idols' Song

We are the shape of things to come,
Born to entertain and have fun.
We hope you like our fun song.
Sing it with us it won't take long.

I'm Triangular Trev, I have three angles,
three straight sides and play the guitar.
My Auntie Polygon says I will go far.
Hope you enjoyed our Band Idol story.
I promise not to take all the glory.

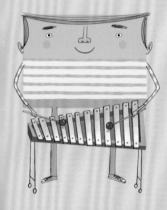

I'm Nonagon Norma, my favourite number is nine.
I sing and play the tambourine to the beat in time.
We are all crazy about numbers, timing and beats,
We like to get everybody moving out of their seats.
We like to add, subtract and sing our times tables too.
Numbers and beats, make it easy to do.

I'm Horizontal Horatio, I sway from left to right.
I love the sound of music playing through the night.
When I play my music, it gets me in the zone.
Especially when I play my epic xylophone.

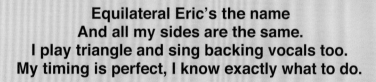

I'm Isosceles Irene, I play the drum and dance to the beat.
You can hear the tapping of my feet.
I have two equal angles and two sides of equal length.
My colourful, positive character goes from strength to strength.

Equilateral Eric's the name
And all my sides are the same.
I play triangle and sing backing vocals too.
My timing is perfect, I know exactly what to do.

I'm Perpendicular Peri, I play the tenor saxophone.
When I play my instrument I never feel alone.
My wonderful shiny instrument of brass has thirty-two keys.
All my friends and family think that I'm the bee's knees.
My favourite shapes are triangles
And two of my lines cross at right angles.

I'm Rectangular Reg with one flat face and four small edges.
With two long and two short sides, I'm hoping to impress the judges.
I play keyboard with eighty-eight keys and stand at the back.
I mix all the instruments together and concentrate on the backing track.

We are the shape of things to come.
You sang with us and had some fun.
We hope to see you again soon
And sing along with our next cool tune!